Angela Throgmorton was exhausted.
The time had come to make a few changes.

Old Tom had been a beautiful baby.

But now he was big enough to help with the housework.

So Angela made a list of things for him to do.

She knew, of course, that it might not be easy to get Old Tom to help.

However, Angela wasn't one to give up.
"Where would you like to start?" she asked nicely.

All of a sudden, Old Tom felt sick.

Angela gave him a kiss and put him to bed.
"Now be a good boy, lie still, and you'll soon get well," she said.
Old Tom had other ideas.

Angela had to dust and wipe and brush and sweep all by herself.

Meanwhile, Old Tom was busy, too.
He had changed into…the Man of Mystery!

Later, in the kitchen, Angela was baking.

But her cooking was interrupted
when she saw fresh fur on her clean floor.

Then Angela heard a noise in the next room.
And saw cake crumbs on the carpet!
"Where could *they* have come from?" she wondered.

Angela paid a surprise visit to Old Tom, with a card and some flowers.

"I do hope you'll be better soon," she said.
"And then you can help around the house."

Angela had worked hard all day. She was tired, and went to bed early —
only to be woken by mysterious footsteps.

Angela decided to investigate.
She followed the footsteps through the house,

and out the window.

The Man of Mystery ran off into the night,

and so did Angela Throgmorton.

She watched as the Man of Mystery called on the neighbours.

"He reminds me of someone," thought Angela.

Then the Man of Mystery stopped for a late-night snack.
Angela moved in for a closer look.

She noticed that the Man of Mystery seemed interested
in a window full of dusters, brushes and brooms.

And when he paused at a restaurant,
Angela thought his manners looked strangely familiar.

In fact, lots of things about this
Man of Mystery were familiar.

Who could it be?

Angela thought she knew.

She hurried home to look in someone's room.

And as she suspected, no one was there.

Angela was waiting when Old Tom came home late.

"So! Too sick to help!" snapped Angela Throgmorton.
The Man of Mystery knew he'd been naughty.
He was sent straight to bed.

Angela couldn't stay cross for long, though.
In the morning, she made a hearty breakfast for Old Tom — he'd be
needing his strength. After all, there was still a long, long list of things for
the Man of Mystery to do around the house.

For Ann Haddon (Jess)
and Ali Lavau

Little Hare Books
4/21 Mary Street, Surry Hills
NSW 2010 AUSTRALIA

A CIP catalogue record for this book is available from the British Library.
ISBN 1 877003 31 X

Designed by ANTART
Produced by Phoenix Offset
Printed in Hong Kong

2 4 5 3 1